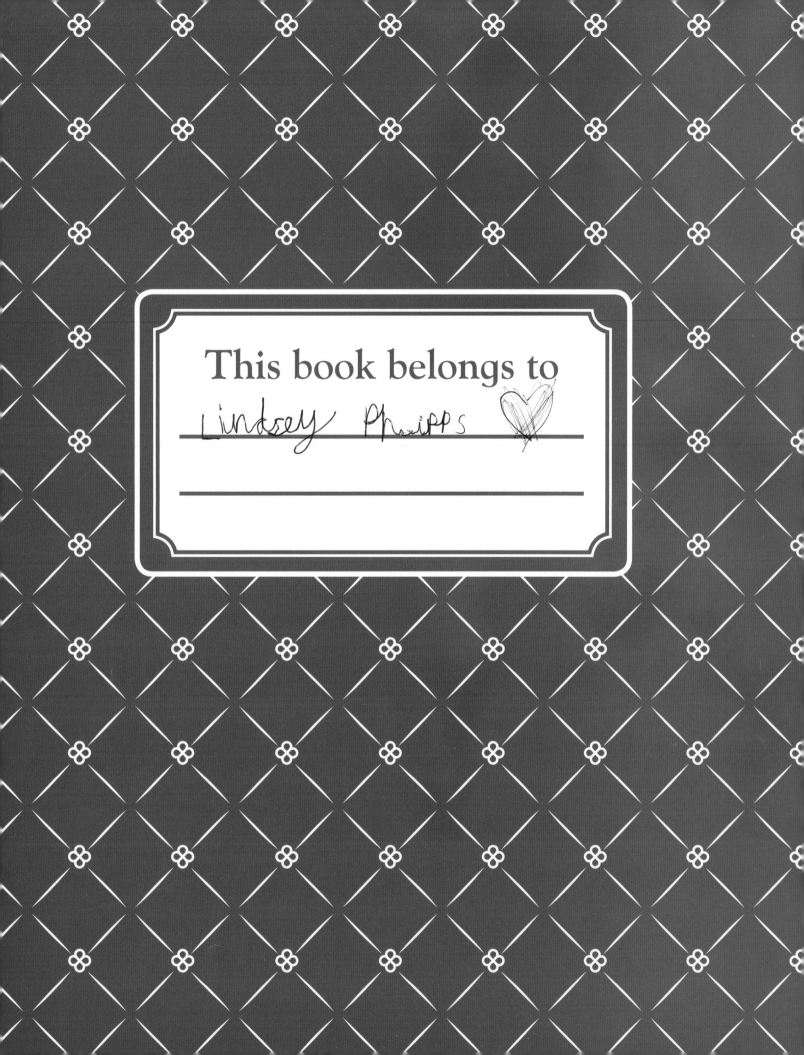

This book belongs to

Lindsey Phillips

This edition published by Parragon Books Ltd in 2014

Parragon Books Ltd
Chartist House
15–17 Trim Street
Bath BA1 1HA, UK
www.parragon.com

ISBN 978-1-4723-8199-6

Printed in China

Disney MOVIE COLLECTION
A SPECIAL DISNEY STORYBOOK SERIES

Snow White

PaRragon

Bath • New York • Cologne • Melbourne • Delhi
Hong Kong • Shenzhen • Singapore • Amsterdam

Once upon a time, there lived a beautiful princess named Snow White. Her stepmother, the Queen, was jealous of Snow White's beauty.

Every day the Queen asked her mirror, "Magic Mirror on the wall, who is the fairest one of all?" Each time the mirror would answer, "You are." But one day the mirror replied, "A lovely maid I see, who is more fair than thee." "It's Snow White!" snarled the Queen.

Snow White was in the courtyard, singing as she
went about her chores.

A handsome young prince was riding by and heard
her lovely voice. He climbed the castle wall to find her
but Snow White was shy and ran up to her balcony.

From the courtyard below, the Prince sang
to Snow White and she listened happily.
She placed a kiss on a friendly dove, who
carried it to the Prince below.

At that very moment, the jealous Queen was plotting against Snow White. She ordered her royal huntsman to take Snow White far into the forest and kill her.

Afraid of angering the Queen, the huntsman took
Snow White into the forest to gather wild flowers.

Snow White kneeled to soothe a baby bird that had
fallen from its nest. "Oh, please don't cry," she said.

As she spoke, the huntsman crept up behind her
with his dagger at the ready.

But the huntsman could not harm the gentle girl.
"Forgive me," he begged. Then he warned Snow White about
the Queen's evil plan. "Run away, child, and never come back!"

Snow White fled into the forest. As she ran, she felt eyes watching her. The trees seemed to reach out to grab her.

With nowhere left to run, she fell to the ground and began to cry.

After a while, Snow White looked up and found herself surrounded by forest animals. "Do you know where I can stay?" she asked them.

The friendly animals led Snow White to a tiny cottage in the woods.

"It's like a doll's house!" said Snow White. She knocked at the door but no one answered. "Please may I come in?" she called. Still, there was no reply.

Slowly she stepped inside.

As Snow White wandered through the house, she discovered seven little chairs and seven little beds.

"Seven little children must live here! Let's clean the house and surprise them," the princess suggested. "Then maybe they'll let me stay."

Close by, the seven dwarfs who owned the cottage were busy working in their mine. All day long they dug for diamonds.

At five o'clock it was time to go. Doc led Grumpy, Happy, Sleepy, Sneezy, Bashful and Dopey home, singing and whistling as they went.

When the dwarfs reached their cottage the light was on – someone was in their house! They crept inside and tiptoed upstairs to find someone fast asleep beneath their blankets.

"It's a monster!" whispered one dwarf.

Stepping closer, Doc cried out, "Why, it's a girl!"
The dwarfs gazed at Snow White.
"She's beautiful," Bashful said. "Just like an angel."

Snow White sat up and said, "How do you do?"
She explained to the dwarfs who she was and
what the evil Queen had planned for her.
"Don't send me away," she begged.

"If you let me stay, I'll wash and sew and sweep and cook," Snow White promised.

At that the dwarfs shouted, "Hooray! She stays!" And the happy princess ran to the kitchen to prepare dinner.

The dwarfs rushed downstairs to eat, but Snow White
said, "Supper is not quite ready. You'll just have time to wash.
Let me see your hands."

They reluctantly showed their dirty hands to Snow White.
"Worse than I thought," she said. "March straight outside and
wash, or you won't get a bite to eat."

All the dwarfs but one headed to the tub. "I'd like to see anybody make me wash!" said Grumpy.

Just as Grumpy spoke, the other dwarfs pounced on him and dumped him into the tub. They scrubbed him squeaky-clean.

"You'll pay for this!" growled Grumpy.

Back at the castle, the Queen stood before her Magic Mirror. "Who is the fairest of them all?" she asked, as usual. But instead of answering as she had expected, the mirror told her that Snow White was the fairest in the land. She was still alive – the huntsman had lied to her!

The mirror also told the Queen exactly where Snow White was hiding.

The angry Queen drank a potion that disguised her as an old hag. Then she created a magic apple. "With one bite of this poisoned apple, Snow White's eyes will close forever," she cackled. "Only a kiss from her true love will wake her!"

Peddler's Disguise,

Formula
Mummy Dust,
Black of Night
Old Hags Cackle
Scream of Fright

Back at the cottage, Snow White and the
seven dwarfs were unaware of the Queen's
plot. They finished Snow White's delicious
dinner and then they sang and danced late
into the night.

Even Grumpy joined the fun, thumping
away on a pipe organ.

The next morning, Snow White kissed each dwarf goodbye
as he marched off to the mine. Dopey even managed to get
two kisses!

Doc warned the princess, "The Queen is a sly one. Beware
of strangers!"

"Don't let nobody or nothing in the house!" Grumpy added.

The Queen, disguised as the old hag, spent
the whole night walking through the forest to
the dwarfs' little home.

She waited in the shadows and watched
the dwarfs leave. Then, slowly, she crept up
to the cottage.

Snow White was busy making a pie when a shadow fell over her. She looked up with a gasp and saw the old lady at the window.

"All alone, my pet?" the Queen asked Snow White. Then she offered the princess the poisoned apple.

"Go on, have a bite."

Snow White's bird friends knew the old woman was not who she claimed to be. Before Snow White could take the apple, the birds dived at the Queen, pecking her hair and flapping their wings in her face, trying to drive her away.

"Shame on you, frightening an old lady," Snow White scolded the birds. She felt sorry for the old woman and helped her inside the cottage.

The birds and forest animals raced to the
diamond mine to warn the dwarfs. They tugged
on the dwarfs' beards and hats. They pulled
their sleeves and pushed them from behind.
At last, the dwarfs understood.

"The Queen! Snow White!" Doc cried.

"We've got to save her!" Grumpy shouted.

But before the dwarfs could get back to the cottage, Snow White took the poisoned fruit from the old lady and took a single bite.

Snow White fell to the ground, dropping the rest of the apple. "Now I'll be the fairest in the land!" cackled the Queen, as a huge thunderstorm began outside.

The Queen ran from the cottage and out into the rain. But before she could escape, the seven dwarfs and all the forest animals came charging at her through the trees.

"There she goes," cried Grumpy. "After her!"

Thunder boomed overhead and lightning struck all around, but the dwarfs kept on chasing the Queen. They climbed after her and cornered her at the top of a rocky cliff. "I'll fix you!" she shrieked as she tried to roll an enormous boulder down on top of them.

Suddenly, a bolt of lighting struck the ledge where the Queen stood!

The rock crumbled beneath her feet and the evil Queen fell from the cliff and into the darkness below.

The heartbroken dwarfs built a beautiful bed for the sleeping Snow White and watched over her day and night. Then one day the Prince appeared in the forest clearing.

The handsome Prince had
searched far and wide for the girl
he had met at the well that
morning. When he came to the
clearing where Snow White lay,
he kneeled down and, with great
sorrow, kissed her farewell.
It was Love's First Kiss!

With a soft sigh, Snow White sat up and rubbed her eyes. The Prince shouted with joy and lifted her in his arms. The dwarfs danced and laughed and the woods rang with calls from the happy forest animals. Snow White was alive!

Snow White thanked the dwarfs for all they had done, then kissed each one goodbye, promising to see them again soon. Together, the Prince and Snow White rode off to his castle, where they lived happily ever after.